Anansi the Spider and the Sky King

A Tale from Africa

SETTINGS

A jungle in Africa;
the vast kingdom of the sky

Anansi: Once upon a time, a brave and clever spider, Anansi, lived with his beautiful wife, Aso, on a huge web. And they lived happily ever after.

Aso: Anansi, that's a terrible story—nothing happened.

Anansi: I apologize, Aso, but I have no exciting stories to share because Sky King owns all the good ones.

Aso: It's unfair that Sky King keeps all the good stories to himself. Do we all not deserve to enjoy tales of magic and heroes?

Anansi: You are absolutely correct. I will go to Sky King and convince him to share the stories with everybody in the world.

Aso: Let's go together.

Aso and **Anansi:** Scurry, scurry, off we go.

Anansi: Sky King, we have traveled for days to reach your palace. There's something we would like to discuss with you.

Sky King: Why should a great king speak with tiny spiders? My kingdom is the sky; you are each just a speck.

Anansi: I beg your pardon. Perhaps I am small in stature, but my strength and determination are great.

Sky King: Well, what is your inquiry, determined spider?

Anansi: I want stories—tales of adventure to share with my wife, my friends, and the world! But all the stories belong to you. I would like to make a deal. Will you share your stories in exchange for something else that you desire?

Sky King: Ha! Remember, as Sky King, everything I desire is available to me. There's nothing a tiny spider could give to someone as great and powerful as me.

Aso: You're absolutely certain?

Sky King: Well . . . now that I have taken a moment to consider the matter, the cost of my collection shall be . . . a python, a leopard, and a swarm of hornets!

Aso: You don't believe that a little spider can pay your enormous price, do you?

Sky King: I believe it's highly unlikely. Good-bye, spiders—and good luck. You'll need it!

Anansi: I'll convince that ill-mannered Sky King to respect me for my abilities and my determination. I'll bring him everything he asked for!

Aso and Anansi: Scurry, scurry to the jungle.

Aso: Capturing a python, a leopard, and a swarm of hornets will be difficult. But we are both clever. I'm certain we'll think of ways to catch them all.

Anansi: Here comes a python now.

Python: Ssssssssss—slither, slither. I am the longest, most feared snake in the world.

Anansi: *(whispering)* He is very long, but he is also very proud. If his pride is his weakness, perhaps we can use that to catch him.

Aso: Good idea. *(loudly)* That python sure looks long to me.

Anansi: Nonsense, that python is considerably shorter than this stick.

Python: What are you two measly spiders arguing about?

Anansi: My wife insists that you are longer than this stick. I disagree.

Python: What?! *Me?* Shorter than a mere stick? You are a ridiculous little spider. Can't you see that I am quite long, and in fact, significantly longer than your stick? I am longer than that tree! I am even longer than the River Nile!

Anansi: I think you're in denial.

Python: If you do not believe me, then I invite you to measure for yourself, silly spider. I'll slither next to your stick to prove my great size. I'm quite a sight when I'm stretched out to my full length.

Anansi: Go ahead. I will lay my stick down here on the ground.

Python: Please observe as I stretch my glorious tail all the way down and *past* the end of the . . . Hey! What are you doing?

Anansi: I'm tying you to the stick for a trip to Sky Kingdom.

Python: Hey! Let me go.

Aso and **Anansi:** Scurry, scurry to Sky King.

Sky King: Ah, Anansi, it appears that you, a miniscule spider, have succeeded in bringing me a python!

Python: Excuse me, your majesty, I'm not just a python. I am an *enormous* python!

Anansi: And remember, *I* am a determined spider. Surely you now respect me, despite my size?

Sky King: I'm not yet convinced. Good luck bringing me a leopard!

Aso: You will have your leopard before long.

Aso and Anansi: Scurry, scurry back to the jungle.

Leopard: *Mrrrrawr!*

Aso: There's a leopard. How will we trap such a ferocious beast?

Anansi: I'm still figuring out a plan. *(louder)* Hello, Leopard!

Leopard: What? Who's there?

Anansi: Two spiders, down here on the ground next to this leaf.

Leopard: Spiders! I despise spiders! I crush spiders with my mighty paws.

Aso: Look out, Anansi! Quick, scurry up the tree!

Leopard: I missed you . . . this time! But I pass this way regularly, and I crush every spider in my path. *Mrrrrawr!*

Aso: That's not exactly polite.

Anansi: No, but it gives me an idea. We will dig a deep hole, cover it with branches, and tomorrow when the leopard comes along, he'll fall into it.

Aso and Anansi: Dig, dig, all day long.

Leopard: Ah, it's another perfectly beautiful day here in the jungle. WHOOOAAA! Where did this hole come from?

Anansi: Leopard, are you hurt?

Leopard: I'm not hurt, but I find myself trapped and extremely annoyed. I cannot believe I'm asking two ridiculous spiders for help, but I need assistance to get out of this hole.

Aso: If we help you out, you'll probably crush us!

Leopard: No! I will not crush you. Help me!

Anansi: Do you *promise* not to crush us, Leopard?

Leopard: I promise that you two silly spiders will be perfectly safe . . . *(quietly)* for now.

Anansi: All right, I'm tossing you a rope. Tie it very tightly around your tail.

9

Leopard: The rope is tied around my tail now.

Anansi: (*quietly*) Aso, I'm tying the other end to this tree branch very tightly. When I say *launch*, you cut the rope and jump on.

Aso: Are you hanging on tightly to the rope?

Anansi: I am. Now . . . Launch!

Leopard: Wheeeee! I'm out of the hole and flying through the sky!

Anansi: We are all flying, Leopard. We're headed straight for the palace of Sky King . . . And now, we are coming in for a landing.

Sky King: Well, what have we here?

Anansi: The second part of your payment: One leopard.

Leopard: One seriously annoyed leopard, that is!

Python: You know, Leopard, I too was very angry when these spiders brought me here. They tricked me!

Leopard: I'm astonished that two tiny, insignificant spiders got the better of me.

Aso: We apologize, Leopard and Python. We hope you'll eventually understand that by coming to Sky Kingdom, you're helping the rest of us. We also hope you will come to respect us for our cleverness and our abilities, and not judge us by our size.

Leopard: I'm still not entirely happy with being tricked, so get out of here before I crush you!

Anansi: I'm moving as quickly as my little legs will carry me. Sky King, we'll be back soon with hornets.

Sky King: I'm beginning to believe that, Anansi.

Aso and **Anansi:** Scurry, scurry back to the jungle.

Hornet: *Buzzzzzzzzz.*

Aso: There they are, Anansi: the hornets. They are nasty little creatures.

Anansi: At least the hornets are about our size, even if they are unpleasant.

Hornet: Excuse me, I couldn't help but overhear that you spiders consider hornets to be unpleasant. We are not at all mean; we are misunderstood. If people and spiders would stop pestering us while we are working, we wouldn't need to sting. That's a hint for you to go away.

Anansi: Don't worry, Hornet, we're just passing by on our way to examine those attractive empty gourds. We won't bother you, so please go about your business.

Hornet: I will. We are especially busy today. We are just beginning to bore through this tree trunk to build a spectacular new nest for ourselves and our queen.

Anansi: Here's the plan, Aso. We'll fill this empty gourd with water, then you will climb up high in the tree with it and pour it over the hornets.

Aso: I understand. They'll think it's raining. They're just starting to build their nest, so they have no shelter yet.

Anansi: My dear wife, you are as clever and cunning as I am.

Aso: Thank you! There, the gourd is full of water now. It's time for the downpour to begin.

Anansi: Good! I'll crouch over here behind the other gourd.

Hornet: What's this? The weather forecast didn't call for rain showers today! We cannot work under these conditions, and we have nowhere to go!

Anansi: Hornet! Come quickly, there is shelter from the downpour inside this dry gourd; there's enough space in here to protect your entire swarm.

Hornet: That's an excellent solution, spider! Hornets, fly to the gourd! Inside, all of you! We will wait for this downpour to end and then we will get back to work immediately!

Aso: All the hornets are inside the gourd, Anansi! Plug the opening with clay and let's hurry back to Sky King!

Hornet: What is the meaning of this? You cannot trap us in here. We have a strict work schedule! Our queen will be cross with you!

Aso: Finally our task is complete! We'll soon have wonderful stories to make our mornings, afternoons, and evenings more enjoyable!

Anansi: Hopefully, we'll also earn Sky King's respect.

Aso and **Anansi:** Scurry, scurry to Sky King.

Sky King: Anansi and Aso, why am I not surprised to see you here again? I suppose you resourceful spiders have my swarm of hornets trapped inside that gourd.

Anansi: You suppose correctly, Sky King. We present to you one swarm of hornets, although I can't imagine what you want with these nasty creatures.

Hornet: We're not nasty, we're misunderstood! We just prefer not to be interrupted when we are working! I will add that being trapped in a gourd is a tremendous interruption. The swarm is now completely off schedule.

Leopard: Relax, Hornet, you're far away from your queen up here in the sky. She'll find some other hornets to do her work for her. Go ahead and enjoy the view. Think of this as a well-deserved vacation.

Aso: Sky King, we have delivered to you one python, one leopard, and a swarm of hornets. You didn't believe that creatures so small would be able to pay your price.

Sky King: Indeed, I regret that I made judgments about your ability based on your appearance. Both of you have truly earned my respect.

Anansi: Thank you. I have kept up my end of the bargain. Will you honor our agreement?

Sky King: My collection of wonderful stories is yours, Anansi. But please promise that you will not keep the stories to yourselves, as I so selfishly did. Share each one with your friends and family, and ask them to do the same. Spread the joy of an entertaining tale throughout the world for the rest of time.

Anansi: Definitely! The first story I'll tell is the one about the spiders and Sky King. When I am done sharing my adventure, I hope that others will tell their stories, too.

Aso: That's a wonderful idea. Everyone scurry, scurry, and tell us: What is *your* story?

The End